MACMILLAN READERS

STARTER LEVEL

POLLY SWEETNAM

Shooting Stars

D1432044

MACMILLAN

Lisa and Alice are friends.
They are on a plane.
They are watching a film.
They are on holiday.
They are going to an island
in Greece.

Look, Alice! There's
Matt Lepardi. He's great!
He's my favourite film star.
Our holiday is starting well.

Matt Lepardi loves Claudia Carman.
She's his fiancée. They are going
to get married. She's a film star too.

This is the Hotel Oracle. Lisa and Alice are going to stay here.

Kostas and Eleni own the Hotel Oracle.
They love their hotel. They like their guests.
They cook wonderful food for the guests.

That was a wonderful meal, Eleni.

Thank you, Lisa.

What can we do on this island?

You can do lots of exciting things. You must visit the Museum. There are beautiful statues in the Museum.

Lisa and Alice are enjoying their holiday. Each day, they swim in the sea. Each day, they eat delicious food.

Today, the girls are in the Museum. A guide is talking about a statue.

Two other tourists are near Lisa and Alice. These tourists are talking about film stars.

Look at this newspaper. Here's a story about Matt Lepardi and Claudia Carman.

They are visiting this island. They are making a film here. They are shooting some scenes here.

7

The next morning the sun is shining brightly.

I'm going to go to the shops. I want to buy some postcards and some souvenirs. Do you want to come, Lisa?

No, thanks. My hair is wet. I'll sit on the balcony. The hot sun will dry my hair.

Lisa is on the balcony. The sun is hot. Lisa looks at the Hotel Astra. It is a big and important hotel.

Then Lisa sees two people. They are on the balcony of the Hotel Astra. The woman is looking at the sea. The man is looking at the woman.

It's Claudia Carman and Matt Lepardi! Claudia is sad. Why? Matt isn't sad. He is angry.

Now Matt is shouting at Claudia. He is angry. Claudia is angry too. She is shouting at Matt.

Lisa can see Claudia and Matt. But she can't hear their words.

Suddenly, Matt pulls Claudia into their room.

Oh no! This is terrible! Matt is hurting Claudia. What shall I do?

Claudia and Matt are in their room. Claudia takes a gun from her bag.

Lisa sees everything.

Lisa hears the sound of the gun. Matt falls onto the sofa.

Claudia is on the balcony. The gun is in her hand. She sees Lisa.

Claudia is looking at me. She has the gun. She is going to shoot me. She is going to kill me!

I must find Kostas and Eleni. They will help me.

Lisa is in the Hotel Oracle's restaurant. But she can't find Kostas and Eleni.

Suddenly, Lisa sees a man and a woman. They are standing by the door.

Please, don't be frightened. We want to talk to you.

Everything is OK. Matt is not dead.

Claudia and I are making a film on the island. In the film, I fight with Claudia. Claudia kills me. We practise our scenes in our hotel room.

The gun is not real. Claudia will never hurt me. I will never hurt her. We love each other very much.

Wow! Claudia Carman and Matt Lepardi are here! They are talking to Lisa!

Lisa is having an exciting adventure. And I have six postcards and some souvenirs!

16